This book belongs to

_____

YOU ARE

One

Sara O'Leary

artwork by

Karen Klassen

Owlkids Books

So much has changed
in just a year.

You are one!

You used to be carried everywhere.

But now you are on the move.
Crawling.
Taking your first steps.

Now that you are one,
you are trying all kinds of new foods.
Some you like to eat.

Some you would rather wear.

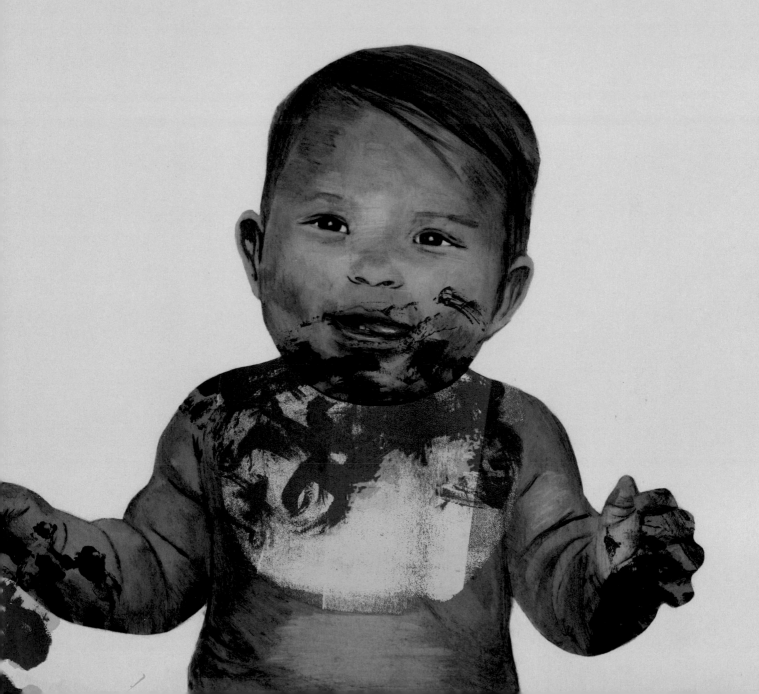

You have perfect little teeth now.
And you did work hard to get them.

You have learned how to ask for things.
When you want a story,
you pick up a book.

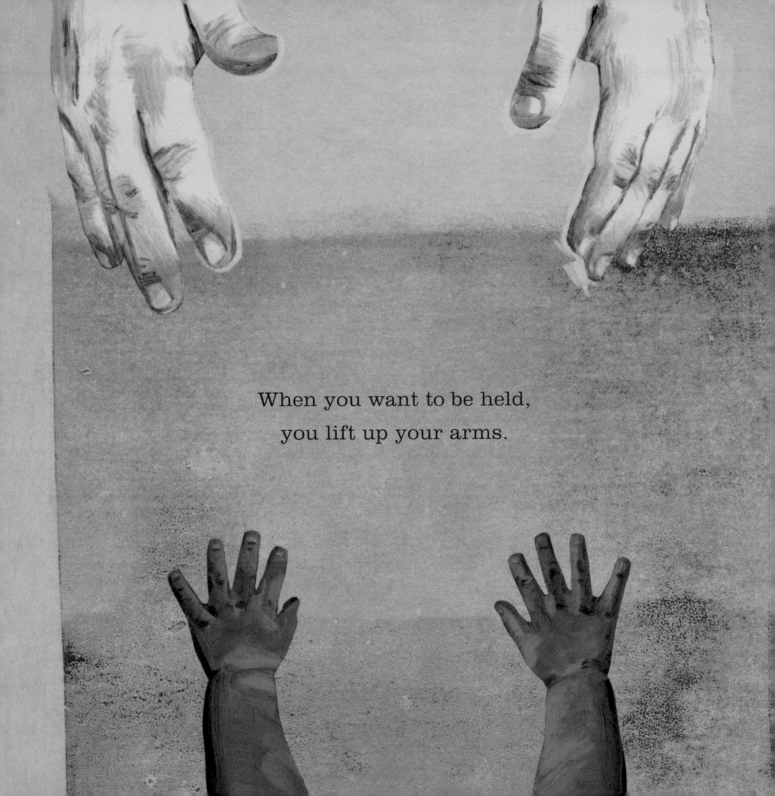

When you want to be held,
you lift up your arms.

You can nod your head for yes,
and shake your head for no,
now that you are one.

And you are very, very good
at the game of peek-a-boo.

You like to play with your toys.
Or sometimes with
the empty boxes they came in.

Your best friend is
the monkey in the mirror.

You like to put things
inside other things.

You hide them.

Then you find them.

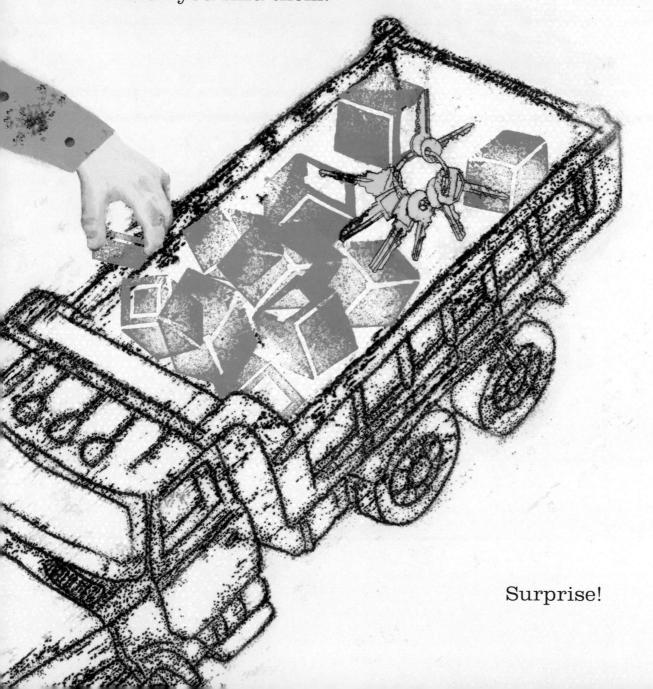

Surprise!

When you are happy,
you can clap your hands.
(And then we all know it.)

You can smile hello,

and wave goodbye.

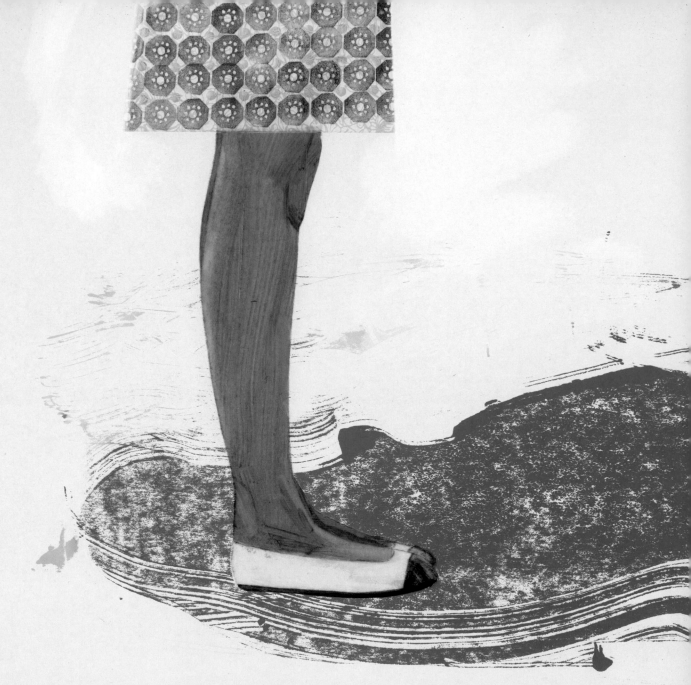

You know your name now.

And you have your own names for us.

You sometimes talk in sentences,
but not always in words.

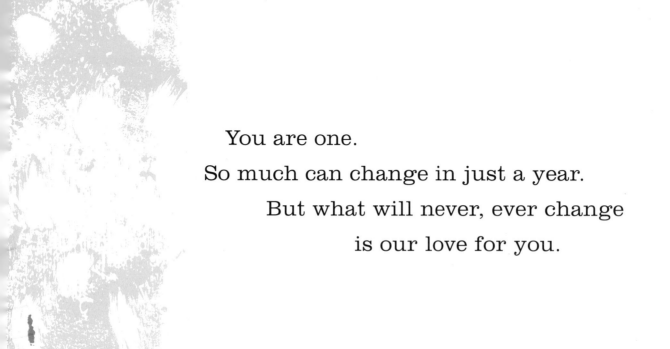

You are one.

So much can change in just a year.

But what will never, ever change

is our love for you.

Owlkids Books acknowledges the financial support of the Canada Council for the Arts, the Ontario Arts Council, the Government of Canada through the Canada Book Fund (CBF) and the Government of Ontario through the Ontario Media Development Corporation's Book Initiative for our publishing activities.

Published in Canada by
Owlkids Books Inc.
10 Lower Spadina Avenue
Toronto, ON M5V 2Z2

Published in the United States by
Owlkids Books Inc.
1700 Fourth Street
Berkeley, CA 94710

Library and Archives Canada Cataloguing in Publication

O'Leary, Sara, author
        You are one / written by Sara O'Leary ; artwork by Karen Klassen.

ISBN 978-1-77147-072-8 (bound)

        I. Klassen, Karen, 1977-, illustrator II. Title.

PS8579.L293Y68 2015   jC813'.54   C2015-905537-7

Library of Congress Control Number: 2015948450

The text is set in Clarendon LT Std.
Edited by: Jennifer Stokes
Designed by: Alisa Baldwin

ONTARIO ARTS COUNCIL
CONSEIL DES ARTS DE L'ONTARIO
an Ontario government agency
un organisme du gouvernement de l'Ontario

 Canada Council   Conseil des Arts
for the Arts   du Canada

Canada

Manufactured in Shenzhen, Guangdong, China, in September 2015, by WKT Co. Ltd.
Job #15CB1194

A   B   C   D   E   F

OWL kids   Publisher of Chirp, chickaDEE and OWL
www.owlkidsbooks.com

Owlkids Books is a division of  Bayard
CANADA